THE

CROWN

AN EAST RIDING CHRISTMAS TALE

CHRIS SPECK

Copyright © 2023 Chris Speck
Flat City Press
All rights reserved.
Front Cover: Skidby Mill by Danny Reed
ISBN: 9781739330873

This is a work of fiction. Unless otherwise indicated, all the names, characters, businesses, places, events and incidents in this book are either the product of the author's imagination or used in a fictitious manner. Any resemblance to actual persons, living or dead, or actual events is purely coincidental.

CHAPTER ONE

Christmas Eve 1721.
The East Riding of Yorkshire.

The snow is knee deep in some places and the wind is sharp. Richie adjusts the pack strapped to his back and looks up at Skidby Hill in the mid-distance, the windmill there is turning slowly and he can just make out the white top. The snow has been on and off all morning and the weather has only cleared a little in the last half an hour. It's just after two, he imagines, although he can't see the sun for the thin clouds. Many miles back, over crisp, snow-covered fields, is the port town of Kingston Upon Hull where he has been on a shopping errand. This is why he carries such a heavy pack that digs into his shoulders.

Richie comes from a little village some eight miles from here called North Burton where there is a stout church, a duck pond, run-down grotty cottages, a well to do manor house and a friendly pub named the Bay Horse. He pulls his threadbare woolly hat over his ears and continues on. It will take him well into the darkness of Christmas Eve to get back home with the goods he carries, and it will be a hard journey in the snow. The trip was Nana's idea. Richie lives in a tatty cottage opposite the Bay Horse with his fat Nana and her swollen legs, she's too old to do much of anything these days except sit in her chair and pass judgement. She can make it across to the pub when there's a free feed, and struggles up to church on Sundays because it's the law to attend. Nana has a gob on her, especially when she's had a drink. A week or so back, there was heavy snowfall - the sort that comes every ten years and blocks the coach roads to Beverley and Market Weighton. It meant that Philipson at the pub wouldn't get some of the things he needed for Christmas, he was expecting dried fruit and plums, salt, rum from the East Indies, and spices to make Christmas Pudding. If the coach can't make it through, then neither can his deliveries. Nana says that an East Riding Christmas isn't proper without pudding on the twenty-fifth after church. Philipson pointed out that the plums and raisins that go inside come from the Indies anyway, and so does the rum – so they aren't really from Yorkshire at all. Philipson wanted to send someone on horseback to Beverley to fetch his stuff but they charge a fortune, and the snow is so thick that a beast wouldn't get through any better than a man. That's when Nana said that Richie would go. If the weather is good, it's a five-hour walk to the busy docks at Kingston Upon Hull. Richie is just seventeen but six-foot-four already and lanky, he's strong from rough farm work and used to the cold or the heat. Nana said it would only take him a day to get to Hull, he could pick up the things Philipson needs, spend a night on the alehouse floor up at the Grey Mare and come back on Christmas Eve; and then Philipson could make his Christmas Pudding after all. 'It'll be good for the lad' said Nana, 'he's built for walking – look at them legs!' The old lass likes to go on and on, 'young folk have gone soft - when I was a lass, I'd think nothing of walking all day, and all night, and I was happy to get out into the fresh air.' Philipson rolled his eyes as he looked down over the bar of the Bay Horse.

So here Richie is, walking a mile away from Skidby Hill with the windmill up ahead in the grey distance. He did spend a night on the alehouse floor, and he did collect the things that Philipson needs for his pudding. Now, he is on the way back. The road has been hard, it's not easy to walk in deep snow when you're carrying so much, at times Richie did not know where he was going, he's not a well-travelled lad. He's already passed through Cottingham, and is on his way back via the little East Riding villages of Skidby, then Walkington, then home. He presses on. Thick snow begins again, sucking all the noise and life from the air. It makes it hard to see. Richie is not really kitted out for this kind of weather – his boot has a hole in the toe and his socks are wet, his jacket is a hand down from the old coachman at the Pennyman Estate, the gloves are woollen like the hat and, if the truth be told, he is struggling in the cold.

At the bottom of the hill before another climb, Richie sees something flapping in the wind on a fence, it's a brown scarf. The snow drives forward into him and he wonders where it's come from, as he steps closer he sees there's a brown boot sticking out of the snow. He's not a thief, but shoes are valuable, even if they're old and despite how cold he is, Richie goes over to it. He squats down and pulls at the heel with his woollen gloves sticky with snow. There's something inside it. It's a foot.

Richie digs at the snow that has gathered on the body with his woollen gloves, he uncovers a buttoned-up waistcoat, and there's a red face with the eyes closed above a well-kept white beard. This old man has a bald head, a thick sheepskin jacket and expensive leather riding gloves. Richie yanks him up out of the snow and he can smell drink. The body is cold but not frozen and red enough to be alive, he sets it against the fence while he thinks what to do. The old man's head rolls to one side, he's passed out drunk perhaps. Richie looks up Skidby Hill where he is headed and back the way he came. The snow is coming down thick, he will have to get this man out of the cold – he shall die if he doesn't. This will be hard, for Richie is already carrying a dead weight of fruit, rum, and dried plums for his Nana – he cannot set these things down and leave them for they will be lost in the snow. What would Nana say? He takes a deep breath. It has been a difficult trip, it looks to get harder yet, but he cannot leave this old man out in a blizzard to freeze up. That's not what a village lad would do. He does one of his big sighs.

Richie drags the body up the hill. With his arms around the man's chest, he pulls him backwards up the steady slope and the brown boots leave two lines in the snow as they go. It's a good job this old fellow isn't very tall. Richie rests every twenty or so yards. To carry the body over his shoulder would cause injury to the old man, and there's the pack on his back as well.

It takes near enough twenty minutes to get to the top of the hill near the windmill, it would take Richie much less than half that without a body to drag. It's deserted. Who would be out in this? Skidby windmill stretches up into the grey blizzard, and the big sails hardly move in the snow with the light wind driving the flakes in a diagonal direction. Richie drags the old man to the side of the tower and sets him sitting down with his back against the bricks. He squats with the body in front of him to think about his next move. Understand that Richie is a tough lad, he ploughs complete fields in spring, harvests and bails hay in the autumn, his hands are wide and strong and he is powerful with big shoulder muscles and a slender back, but, in the cold and with the wrong sort of clothes, carrying the pack and having charge of some old man who is about to die, he is worried and fatigued. There's the creeping sensation in Richie's head also, that if he doesn't get out of the snow and the cold soon, he might end up like the old man he carries, and then they will both be dead. His feet are frozen and his hands raw in the tatty woollen gloves.

He struggles on, dragging the man down the lane and around the corner into the little village of Skidby. The snow is thick in places and his feet make holes as he struggles to pull the body. He looks along the little street with a jumble of cottages in stages of disrepair, their thatched roofs are heavy with snow and lines of smoke snake out the chimneys into the grey, fuzzy sky. Richie will have to bang on someone's door – he does not want to do this, like his Nana says, Jacksons can look after themselves. He continues down the street backwards and the weight of the old man is beginning to hurt him. Raised off the road to the right is a stout white building with a low roof and bright lights in the windows. This is the inn, the sign swings in the wind displaying the name: the Half Moon. Richie has never been here, but he already knows what's behind the black door, there will be cold and hard faces for a stranger, especially a stranger in distress in the dead of winter, and at Christmas time as well. The folk fear the unknown round here, but Richie cannot go on much longer, and, he cannot let this old man die.

With the last of his effort, he drags the body across the road to the lights of the pub. It is a wretched situation. Richie leans his head against the black door and bangs on it with the fat of his hand. In a minute there's the sound of the bolts sliding across from the other side, and the latch opens to the face of a thin young woman dressed in an apron and a long blue skirt. Just as Richie imagined, she has a face of cold stone with a pointed nose and keen eyes. She looks at Richie with a frown and then down to the old man he carries.

"By God," she bellows, "Father!"

It's too warm for Richie. He's been ordered to go through the lounge and told to sit in a wooden chair in front of the fire in the kitchen. The old man he carried has been dumped in an armchair opposite by the thin woman who opened the door – turns out she is the Landlord's daughter. A large hearth dominates one wall of the kitchen and there's a long wooden table in the centre of the room, it's rough and uneven with use and stacked with plates, bread rolls, knives and forks, wooden cups and an open sack of flour. The fire crackles and sends flickering shadows onto the stone walls and ceiling beams above. It's not night yet, but dark outside. On a spit beside the flames is a joint of beef, fat rolls off into the pan below. It's a way off being ready yet. On the mantelpiece above is a tatty holly wreath, it is Christmas Eve after all.

"Where did you find him?" asks the thin woman. She has sharp blue eyes and a hooked but petite nose.

"At the bottom of the hill," he answers.

"He's a stubborn old bastard," she says, "he left a few hours ago on horseback for the docks at Hull. I told him the snow was too bad."

"He must have fallen, I didn't see a horse," says Richie.

"Aye, or worse. Someone could have pulled him off and clobbered him." The old man's thin face looks serene and red as he sits there with his eyes closed. "I'm sorry says the lass, I'm Mrs Turner – this is my father, the Landlord. Who are you, lad?" She has a kind eye for him already.

"Richie Jackson of North Burton, Mrs. I'm delivering this package back home for Christmas Eve." He nods to the pack that is still fixed to his back.

"You won't make it in this snow," she says.

"I'll have to," replies Richie. She can see his nose and cheeks are red from the cold.

"Where've you come from?"

"Kingston Upon Hull."

"All that way, in this, on foot?" Her face is creased with worry.

"Aye. Will the old man be alright?"

"I think so. God saves drunks. When he left earlier, he was three sheets to the wind," she means he was tanked up. "If you'd left him there, he'd be dead for sure." Mrs Turner stands in front of him and he can see her clearly. She's in her twenties and has a smooth, worried face, she's possibly too young to be a landlady but there's a capable sense about her. It's clear from the way she acts that she runs this place and will have situations to deal with all the time, perhaps that's why she's gruff and to the point. "You sit by the fire a minute, get yourself warm."

"Aye. I'll just catch my breath," says Richie. Mrs Turner looks down at him, at the battered shoes he wears and the thin scarf around his neck. He's lucky he isn't already frozen to death. She shakes her head.

"You'll have to stay here, at least until morning."

"I must get these supplies to my Nana and Philipson from the Bay Horse by tonight. Christmas won't be the same without it. I'm under orders." Richie worries about getting things wrong, and despite his size, upsetting people he loves unnerves him.

"Listen to me, Richie Jackson from North Burton, your Nana will not want you dead on Christmas Day, I can promise you that." Richie sighs. Mrs Turner goes back to her father, she removes his sheepskin jacket, takes off the waistcoat and the boots as well as the gloves. She gathers a fur blanket from the line of coat hooks on the far wall, and like he was a baby, tucks him up in it, so that just his red face and head stick out the top. The old man looks content. He'll be warm enough, especially next to this fire. She turns to Richie.

"You'll have to stay here," she repeats. He sees worry in her sharp blue eyes. "Have you worked in a kitchen before?" she asks. Richie takes off the woollen hat because he's already beginning to sweat.

"Aye," he says. Richie has hung around the kitchen at the Bay Horse plenty of times, he's carried firewood, watched Philipson cook, swept the floors, cut potatoes – not so much now he is older and he's more likely to be drinking, but he knows a pub kitchen even if he's not a cook. He turns his head to look around, and something is missing in the room. In one corner there's a large wooden cupboard standing tall, crammed with jars of pickles, preserves, and dried herbs, there's a goose already plucked hanging from one of the shelves on a hook. There are pans, sacks of sugar and flour on the floor, rolls of freshly made bread covered in tea towels sit on the table. It's food enough for Christmas, but there's nobody here. Richie looks back to Mrs Turner.

"Where's the cook and the serving lasses?" he asks. She blinks at him and swallows.

"My father here is the cook, Richie, as am I. There were meant to be two girls coming from Cottingham this morning, but the snow has been too bad for them to get here. I have two coaches in who are to spend Christmas Day here. They stayed last night and were meant to be well on their way back to York now but the weather trapped them here at Skidby. I've been tasked with feeding them and making sure they have as fine an East Riding Christmas as can be had." Richie sees the worry in her eyes.

"How many?"

"There are twelve of them, two families, the Allgoods out of Northumberland and the lord of the manor himself Mr Bentley - it's he who donated that side of beef over the fire."

"And just you to cook and serve?"

"There's Auntie Bramble here as well." A tiny hunched old woman moves into the kitchen with a bucket of firewood in one of her wrinkled hands. She faces the floor and her eyes are cast down, there's the mist of a simpleton over her as she approaches the fire. Richie watches as the frail lass sets the bucket on the hearth and slowly reaches down to collect a mid-sized log to put it between the flames. She is achingly slow. "Auntie is quicker in the summer, Richie Jackson," says Mrs Turner. She has the same kind of dry humour that Richie is used to.

"There's just two of you to feed all those mouths?" he asks.

"Aye, and feed them well."

"I'd crack open the finest barrel of ale there is in the bar room," says Richie, "give each their own mug and they can drink till tomorrow." Mrs Turner's face becomes serious. This is not the Bay Horse. The families that Mrs Turner has to feed are well-to-do, rich and educated with it. The Allgoods divide their time between the capital and Northumberland where they have extensive lands. Mr Bentley owns the whole village here including the pub, the farms and all the better cottages along one side of the main street.

"I'm afraid it is a matter of pride and fortune for me and mine," says Mrs Turner. "Mr Bentley has promised the

Allgood family they will be as well fed as they can be. He's given the beef and brought brandy from his own kitchens."

"It can't be done," says Richie with a grin. He's used to the easy ways of the Bay Horse and Miss Pennyman's farm.

"It has to be," she says. "Mr Bentley will throw my father and I out into the street boxing day if we fail – that's why he drank a bottle of brandy this morning and took off on the best horse we had. He'd had enough, although he won't remember it when he wakes up." Richie puts his still wet woollen hat back on his head; suddenly the bitter cold outside doesn't seem so bad. "Will you help me?" says Mrs Turner, he can see the proud face does not want to ask such a question. "At Christmas time, you would be doing charity for me, Sir. I need someone to help me run this kitchen, just for the beef meal this evening - then you'd be done." Richie has never been called 'Sir' before. He does not want to upset Mrs Turner, she has a pleasant, if sensible way about her.

"I have to get these things back to my Nana," he pleads.

"I do not know your Nana, Richie, but I am sure she would counsel you to stay and help a poor woman in need."

"You don't know my Nana," he answers.

"The weather is too bad, even a big lad like you will catch your death. Please. For my father, and for me, for Auntie Bramble here also. If Mr Bentley puts her out on the street, she'd die before the sun set over the fields."

"A man wouldn't do that," says Richie.

"You don't know Mr Bentley," she answers. Richie does not have to meet Mr Bentley to know what kind of a man he is – you can find such slave drivers all over the East Riding. Auntie Bramble looks at Richie with her wide, pale eyes and her lips tight over hollow gums, she has a lonely expression and sunken, wretched cheeks. He sighs. Richie is a soft touch. Mrs Turner holds her palms together as if she is begging. Her eyes are watery. How can Richie refuse?

"I'll help," he says.

Mrs Turner is a no-nonsense landlady and cook. She has Richie sat on a stool in front of a sack of potatoes, he's been asked to peel them. She watches to see if he can do it and sees that although he's not a novice, he doesn't have a real cook's skill. It's good enough. At least he is faster than bumbling Auntie Bramble. The joint of beef over the fire on a spit is starting to cook slowly, in between cutting up carrots, Auntie Bramble turns the handle with her thin hands. The kitchen is hot and Mrs Turner disappears at intervals to deal with the front of house, there's noise coming from down the hall and the lounge where the Christmas guests must be gathered. Richie peels potatoes and looks at the man he rescued earlier sleeping peacefully in the tatty armchair by the fire with a red face and serene closed eyes. He thinks of the items he is meant to get back to North Burton by today, and how cross his Nana will be. Richie takes a deep breath, this village of Skidby might be eight miles only from North Burton, but he doesn't know them here – why should Richie get into trouble for them, he has, after all, just saved Mrs Turner's father from freezing to death in the cold? He peels one more spud and stands, goes to the wooden back door, and opens up. The world outside is pure white, with snowflakes the size of guineas falling in muffled silence. He takes a gasp of air and needles of cold prickle the inside of his lungs. Even if he had proper boots to walk in, and a heavy woollen cloak, he would not get through this before nightfall. Richie is trapped. He closes the back door to the cold.

Mrs Turner enters the kitchen and her nostrils are flared under the keen eyes. She has the manner of a schoolteacher.

"There's wood needed in the lounge, Richie," she snaps. "There's plenty in the shed out back." She eyes him and is about to add the same harsh words she uses on Auntie Bramble when she realises that this tall lad is not here to be shouted at. She adds, "if you please," at the end of the sentence. Auntie Bramble looks up in shock.

CHAPTER TWO

The lounge is hot and stuffy, this is good on a snowy late afternoon like today. There's a little curved bar of brown mahogany and steps that lead down from the kitchen door behind it. Mrs Turner keeps bottles of ale in crates on the floor here, there are tankards hung up from hooks over the shelves and bottles of apple brandy and port below. This isn't a posh pub but the clientele today are much more well-to-do than usual farm workers or the lads who work up at the mill. In the lounge room in front of the bar is a long bench table under the bay window, there are seated perhaps ten people, mostly women with their hair up in buns and dresses that are not the best ones they own by any means. There's an older man at the head of the table with a ruby red coloured cloak over his shoulders and bushy grey white sideburns. This is Isaac Allgood, a man who owns lands far north of here in Hexham, Northumberland, he has a ruddy face and a serious countenance. Standing at the bar are two tall men– not as tall as Richie, but much better dressed. These two are the Bentleys, the shorter bald one is the father and he has a white neck scarf and a blue coat with shiny buttons over his fat gut. His son is tall and slim, perhaps a little younger than Richie with the look of his father but ginger. They have glasses of port, the elder is beetroot faced already and leans on the bar with one of his elbows. He sees Richie struggle down the steps with a bucket of logs:

"By heck," he says, "who the hell are you? There's not many taller than the Bentleys round these parts." Richie tries not to look at the man because this would be rude.

"Richie Jackson of North Burton, Sir" he answers as he walks through the hatch in the bar and carries the bucket over to the fireplace. Richie knows how to address his betters, even if his Nana says they aren't really better than anyone.

"What are you doing in Skidby?" ask the man. As is

fashionable for a person who has a certain amount of wealth, Mr Bentley does not need to be especially civil to someone as badly dressed as Richie. Working lads such as he are little better than the animals in the yard and are actually worth less than a half decent horse or a good breeding bull.

"I'm Mrs Turner's worker today, Sir," says Richie. There's no need to mention that he found the Landlord nearly dead in the snow earlier – he knows this would just cause more trouble. Richie dips his head in deference, then begins to add logs to the low fire from the bucket. The two men at the bar watch him work with the air of those who could easily do it themselves, but can't quite be bothered.

"She's to prepare my guests a fine beef supper," says Mr Bentley, "the like of which you'd find in any country house in the East Riding of a Christmas." He directs his comment to the old man who sits at the head of the table with the dark ruby cloak, he looks up from under bushy eyebrows and does not seem bothered. Clearly this is someone who Mr Bentley wants to impress. Richie builds the fire and grabs the bellows to make the flames lick up around the icy logs – he should leave them in front to warm up a little first but he'd rather not wait. Richie already doesn't like Mr Bentley, and the less time he spends in the man's presence, the better.

"Turn around then, lad," says Mr Bentley to Richie. "Let's have a look at you." With reluctance that does not show, for this would be insolence, Richie stands and turns to face Mr Bentley and his son. They are at once shorter than he is by a good few inches, Richie blinks down at them with his thick brown hair almost touching the rafters. "What did your mother feed you on?" bellows Mr Bentley, his cheeks and nose have the red hue of someone who drinks. Richie doesn't like to say his mother died giving birth to him some seventeen years previous, and that he is a bastard.

"My Nana fed me anything she could get her hands on, Sir, same as any lad in North Burton." A good answer, for

Bentley's question is rhetorical and will only lead him to be able to deliver more comments at Richie's expense.

"How old are you?"

"Seventeen, Sir." This seems to please Bentley.

"My lad, Robert here is just sixteen, and he's got another year of growing, I imagine he'll catch you up. He'll be twice the man you are already I should think. Can you read?"

"No, Sir." Bentley scoffs again at this by blowing air through his lips.

"You won't be able to count either." This is an insult of course, but Richie cannot let it land as such, for although he doesn't know Bentley, the man is clearly someone of merit in this reasonably crowded pub on Christmas Eve.

"I can count enough," answers Richie. When it comes to cards and money on the table, he's as good as any.

"This young fellow here, my Robert, why I'd say he's twice the man you are, perhaps three times." Bentley nods to his boy next to him who looks back at Richie with embarrassed eyes. "You'll have to come back here next year, lanky, and you'll see that our Robert will have grown taller than you." The man is a little drunk, perhaps, or maybe he is just an arse. Richie looks at Robert with his ginger hair swept to one side and his awkward expression of shame for his father.

"Merry Christmas," says Richie. "I'm to help Mrs Turner." He nods his head in a kind of bow as he moves towards the steps that lead to the kitchen. This is a good move.

Auntie Bramble stands at the end of the kitchen table with her head down looking at her feet, her hunched back sticks up higher than her head. She's in trouble for something. Opposite and with her face glowing in anger is Mrs Turner. She would be shouting if they didn't have so many guests so close. As it is, she whispers through gritted teeth at the old woman below her:

"You stupid old cow," she hisses. "You were meant to

collect the fish yesterday morning." Little Auntie Bramble looks down at the floor yet and her face burns. Mrs Turner notices Richie approaching, she appraises him of the dilemma in angry whispers not directed in his direction. "She was meant to get the cod fish from Greenwoods, Cottingham, yesterday morning, and she's forgotten. It's too far to get them now with the snow outside. There won't be enough food." Mrs Turner is not naturally mean, but the stress of the situation is getting to her. Richie nods to the big joint of beef on a spit next to the fire dripping grease.

"There's plenty there," he says.

"Not for twelve of them, Richie Jackson, it's half fat as it is." He frowns at this.

"Philipson, the landlord at the Bay Horse would feed twenty from a piece of beef like that, with other bits and bobs." Even Auntie Bramble looks up at him now with quizzical eyes.

"These are not poor folk, Richie. They won't eat simple pottage like we do. My father was to make a starter of bread and butter with cod's head – nothing fancy, I was to boil them up. There's no point now is there, not without any bloody fish." Cod is expensive – this is food that Richie does not get to eat. Mrs Turner is flustered. He wants to help:

"It's customary for Philipson to feed diners up with a dripping pudding first to swell their stomachs," he explains. Mrs Turner wrinkles her nose. "It saves on meat, and with a rich gravy, why it can satisfy even the fat coachmen from the estate. My Nana calls it Yorkshire Pudding." Auntie Bramble looks up to her employer in confusion, and Mrs Turner does a kind of sarcastic moon grin at the lad.

"This is the East Riding of Yorkshire," she says in her most blunt voice that she reserves ordinarily for Auntie Bramble or the most stubborn drunks. "It's 1721. We serve traditional food here and that's what Mr Bentley expects." Richie is worried that he's stepped out of line. He just wants to help:

"I've seen Philipson do it enough times," he says. "Do you have tins for making bread?" he asks. Mrs Turner nods and points. There beside the fire is a stack of them, they are oblong metal trays where Auntie Bramble will make loaves. Richie moves closer to the fire and the two follow. Cooking places such as this one in a traditional kitchen are made with a metal arm that swings into the fire, in front there's the big joint of beef that is spitting and cooking from the heat, the fat that drips from it is caught in a tray underneath.

"We'll need eggs, flour and a little bit of water," says Richie. He's not an accomplished chef but he knows how this is done. It seems like Mrs Turner is coming round to Richie's suggestion.

"Are you sure you can make them?" she asks. "If we get this wrong, Master Richie, my father and I will be put out into the snow tomorrow, and I think that will kill him." She looks over at the bald man sleeping in the armchair beside the fireplace. There's a look of terror in her eyes. Without her father or a husband, she is at the mercy of society. It's a cruel world.

"I'll do the best I can," says Richie. He has never been called 'master' before and it's a strange feeling. He is worried for Mrs Turner also, for now he has met Mr Bentley and seen the kind of man he is, he knows that everything she has said about him is true.

"I must serve in the lounge," she says. "You shall wear a crown one day, Richie Jackson of North Burton. God will see you are paid for your help this Christmas." He's heard this kind of comment before, and it actually means he won't get paid anything until he's dead and in heaven. She hurries out the room to the lounge where the guests will need their tankards of ale and glasses of port wine topped up, even though they could easily do this themselves.

Richie is a messy cook – he cracks a dozen and a half eggs

into a big bowl with several fistfuls of flour, a bit of water and salt. Philipson says that salt makes cooking mistakes taste good. He whisks this up like he's seen his Nana do, albeit on a smaller scale, bits of flour and egg splatter his pants and shirt. When he's done, he lets the batter rest while he gets the loaf tins ready – all twelve of them. With a big spoon, he scoops dripping fat from the tray under the beef into each one and sets them in the fire with a cloth to stop his hand getting burned. He needs the fat to be smoking hot for this to work. Auntie Bramble cuts onions to make the rest of the beef grease into gravy, she goes at it slowly with her shivering thin old hands. Richie waits until he thinks he can see the oil smoking, takes the trays out from the fire and then, he leans in and pours the batter into the trays with the hot oil – this is how Philipson does it. He sets them back into the hottest places in the fire. They usually take about twenty minutes. Mrs Turner enters the kitchen. She's flustered, again.

"Mr Bentley wants to see you in the lounge, Richie," she says. He frowns in confusion.

"Why?"

"God knows, he was going on about you being taller than his lad, Robert. He's not a pleasant man, Richie. I said you were busy but he was insistent." Richie wipes his hands down with a cloth and goes to the door. Mrs Turner stops him before he goes and knocks some of the flour off his shirt with the back of her hand. "I don't know how I shall get through this day," she says.

"You'll have to come and live with me and my Nana if it all goes wrong," he answers. "Just don't touch those Yorkshire Puddings until I get back." Richie never took himself for a leader but it suits him as he looks at the thin, clever face of Mrs Turner with her big blue eyes. She gives him a weak smile.

In the lounge, Mr Bentley is still standing at the bar and his face is rosier still from the drink. His tall and ashamed lad stands in front of him yet. Bentley sets his glass down on the bar when he sees Richie.

"There he is, look at the bloody size of him, Robert. Come over here lad," Bentley is a little more drunk than when Richie saw him earlier. When he speaks, little bits of spittle fly from his mouth and his neck scarf is at an angle. "Stay that side of the bar, you lanky sod, that's it, stand so you're facing Robert." Richie does as he's asked and stands opposite Mr Bentley's son with a confused face. "Have you heard of Indian arm wrestling before?" he asks.

"No, Sir, I have not," says Richie. He doesn't look directly at Robert over the bar – this would be rude, but he can sense the young man is uncomfortable at his boorish and overbearing father. There is to be some sort of contest.

"Robert's an expert at it, isn't that right, son?" Robert nods. "Well go on then, show him." Robert removes his jacket and hangs it on one of the hooks under the bar. He rolls up the sleeve on one arm of his floppy shirt, and sets his bare right elbow on the wood in front of Richie with his hand sticking up.

"It's from the Americas – it's a game to test strength." Robert's voice is clear, if a little timid, but he's polite at least. "You grab my hand and we see who can force the other's down onto the bar." This is simple arm wrestling, and Richie did not know that it was from as far away as the colonies in the Americas. He's done it a plenty with Jonny Low back at the Bay Horse – Richie is a strong lad and it's a game he's good at.

"Do you want to wrestle now?" asks Richie with incredulity. It's not a game for polite society.

"Aye, lad," says Bentley. "You may be taller, but my lad Robert, he'll be stronger, you mark my words well."

That's what this is all about then. Richie could easily ask why, but he already knows. The reason is clear, it's to show that Richie is not as good as his son. There really is no point in a contest – one look at Robert and anyone can see that he's better dressed, better fed, cleaner and more handsome than tall farm lad Richie Jackson with his tatty clothes and messy, elflocked hair. Mr Bentley starts up again:

"It's Christmas, lad, do you not play games where you come from? Where was it again? Bishop Burton?"

"North Burton, Sir."

"Well then, let's see if your North Burton has got as much strength as our Robert from Skidby has?" Richie does a half sigh. His sleeves are already rolled up and he thinks about the dripping puddings that even now are in the open fireplace behind him. He hopes they're not burning, so he'll have to make this quick. Richie assumes the position and rests his elbow on the smooth wood of the bar. His hand clasps around Robert's in front of him. As soon as their palms touch – Richie knows he will win, easily. Robert's skin is smooth and the hands are without calluses, the grip is soft and the bones are weak within. Robert may be much better fed and dressed than Richie, but he has not spent many hours working with a wooden spade, he's never held a scythe or bailed a field of hay. The young man's hand is almost like kindling in Richie's big grasp. Mr Bentley takes hold of the top of their fists clasped together and tests that both lads are tense.

"Begin," he calls, bits of spittle fly from his mouth, again. They take the strain and Richie feels young Robert's arm stiffen up. He looks up into the lad's eyes and sees the embarrassment of having to do this, just so his father can win against a poor working lad. Richie is a card player and this has taught him much about the nature of games, and of winning and losing. He could beat Robert, easily and humiliate him in front of his father – but how would that help Richie? In some games, the way to win is to lose, for the real game of life is much bigger than an arm-wrestling match on a winter's day at the Half Moon pub, Skidby. Richie does not need to beat Robert, there are wider and more important things to him, the

Yorkshire Puddings even now in the hot flames of the fire, the goods he will not be able to deliver to North Burton, Nana's shouting chest when he arrives late, Mrs Turner keeping her home.

Richie puts on a reasonable show, he moves Robert's hand to the side and then allows the lad to push him back to the centre. Mr Bentley offers words of encouragement, and Robert puts all of himself into it, edging Richie down onto the dark wood of the bar. He beams back at Richie with straight white teeth when he's won.

"I knew it," says Mr Bentley. "He's as strong as a bull is my Robert. That bloody showed you, didn't it?" he gloats with a nasty grin. Richie makes sure he doesn't stare at Mr Bentley too long – that would be rude. "Now what about this meat supper, Mrs Turner!" he bellows.

In the kitchen, Richie has just caught the Yorkshire Puddings in time. He yanks the first loaf tray from the flames and sets in on the table in front of Auntie Bramble – she looks shocked. The batter has risen up the side of the medium loaf tray to form a thick golden brown crust. Richie taps one out onto the counter, it's a wonderful brick of goodness.

"We fill these up with that gravy, Auntie Bramble, and there we are – they're called Yorkshire Puddings." Mrs Turner sets out twelve plates and Richie loads each one with a giant Yorkshire Pudding. They add chopped and boiled carrots, mashed potatoes with cream and butter, parsnips cooked in beef dripping, more potatoes par boiled and then roasted, boiled sprouts and finally, Mrs Turner takes a big knife to the joint of beef that has been resting at the far end of the table. She cuts off huge slices of the tender meat. Auntie Bramble adds gravy and then they are ready.

It takes Mrs Turner a couple of minutes to deliver the meals through to the guests, she doesn't want any help from Richie because he looks too dirty to be working with the food and Auntie Bramble is too slow. She returns to the kitchen and waits by the door looking through the crack at her guests in the lounge. Mrs Turner has her thumb to her teeth in worry. A normal dinner for these rich folks may be several courses – there could be three platters of different fish, three of various types of game, potted larks, shin pies, lemon biscuits, China oranges and all manner of ingredients and spice from around the world. Having all your food on just one plate is very working class, but Mrs Turner has done all she could do with what she has. She waits a few minutes before going back in to fill up their glasses and poke the fire, and when she returns she has a grin on her face. The guests approve of their dinner.

"The dripping pudding worked well, Richie," she says. "Mr Allgood announced that the food was rich and honest, as cooked in any stout Yorkshire kitchen of merit." She is all smiles and her blue eyes twinkle in the light from the kitchen fire. "You saved the day, Richie," she adds. He shrugs his shoulders and his face is wet with sweat from the kitchen and the fire.

"I have to be off now, Mrs Turner," says Richie. He knows the weather was bad before, but maybe it's better now. "It's Christmas Eve, and if I don't make it back to North Burton in time for Christmas Dinner, my Nana will throttle me." Mrs Turner pulls back one of the chairs from the farmhouse table and flops down into it with a mixture of exhaustion and relief.

"You daft bastard," she says, "have a look outside. The snow has started up again." Richie goes to the back door of the kitchen like he did earlier in the day, opens up and looks outside. It's dark already, and the cold is refreshing; great flakes of snow fall in from the swirling wind and the sky is dull and starless. It would actually be madness to try to walk back to North Burton in this.

When Richie returns to the table, there's a half mug of brandy waiting for him. Auntie Bramble has a thimble full in a tiny glass and Mrs Turner has a glug in a tankard.

"That's twenty-year-old brandy in there, Richie," she says. "You've bloody earned it." He picks it up and takes a sniff, the fumes burn his eyes.

"I should be in North Burton," he says.

"I'll write your Nana a letter," answers Mrs Turner. Richie wrinkles his nose.

"She can't read."

"You'll have to get someone else to read it to her."

"She'll just say it's a lie."

"I don't imagine you're a bad lad, Richie. Surely, she'll forgive you."

"Aye, she will, but I'll have to weather a storm first."

"You don't need to go back there, you know." Mrs Turner takes a sip on her brandy. It has been a long while since she's had anyone capable to lean on. The relief makes her say something she knows she ought not to. "You could stay here." Richie is unsure what this serious, slim woman means. "There'd always be a place for you in this kitchen," she continues, "I could use a man's help. I mean it. Stay here - work for me."

There's a rasping cough from behind them and a voice that's unfamiliar. Richie turns to see the man he rescued from the snow many hours previous, now standing, shaky next to his armchair. His face is still red but now his eyes are open, they have a yellow colour to the whites, in his hand is a short single shot flintlock pistol held pointing upwards at Richie's chest. There's insanity to the Landlord as he snarls low through two rotten front teeth:

"You get away from my daughter," he whispers. Richie's face flushes with hot blood, his heart begins to flutter and his stomach rumbles. This is the first time he has had such a weapon pointed at him. In time to come, it will be a common occurrence, right now, however, Richie is confused as well as scared – he's not important enough for someone to want to kill, especially not with a bullet from a gun.

"Set that bloody pistol down, father." This is Mrs Turner bellowing at her old man.

"I'll not," he calls back. "I'll put this bastard thieving Pirate out of his misery for what he's done to you. It's incredible to me that he's come back… it was Christmas last year…"

"You're a blind, tanked up fool," yells Mrs Turner. "Who do you think this is?"

"Your husband, Thomas, the Pirate, come back to steal as much as he can before he's off again."

"He's got two eyes, you drunk arse, it's not Thomas. This is a young lad from North Burton, look at him closer, you bloody fool." The gun wavers, the Landlord lowers the pistol and narrows his eyes at the tall figure. His shoulders relax and he lets his hand fall when he realises that this lad is way too tall, and Thomas was nicknamed 'the Pirate' because he had a patch over his lost eye.

"I've got a thumping headache," he whispers as if he were a child. There's no apology.

"Sit yourself down, father," says Mrs Turner all calm like a mother. "This lad pulled you out of the snow earlier. Without him, you'd be frozen to death in a bush next to the lane. You took off at ten this morning after a skinful, and he brought you back." The man looks dreadful with yellowing, jaundiced, still drunken eyes as he sits back down into the armchair.

"It might be better if I'd just been left there," he says in a moment of clarity.

"Better for you, maybe," says Mrs Turner. "If there's no man in this pub with me, Mr Bentley will toss me into the street as certain as cows eat grass." This is true. A pub requires a landlord in this day and age – even if he does none of the work. Indeed, nothing is allowed to run without men to supervise, Mr Bentley has a big farmhouse at the bottom of the hill and were it not for the serving girls, his wife, his son and two intelligent daughters, the whole thing would fall into disrepair. Bentley, like the Landlord here comes from a line of men whose lives are completely managed for them, like conceited, impotent, and needy gods.

"I'll just have a drink," says the Landlord, "and then I'll be back to myself – you'll see. Then, we'll sort that supper for Mr Bentley and his guests."

"It's been seen to, father," says Mrs Turner. She looks at Richie with the mug of twenty-year-old brandy in his hand and her eyes are apologetic. He senses her unease and passes her the drink which she holds out to her father. In shaking hands, he takes it and puts it to his lips; like the liquid is fresh water, he glugs it up and a line of the golden brandy rolls down the side of his moustache. He grins. This is the way the world works, as Richie understands it – those that do the toil are not important enough to reap the rewards. Sense returns to the older man's eyes as the brandy gets to work on him. Mrs Turner turns back to Richie. She's earnest.

"He is a good man," she says, "you will see when he is himself, and you'll be glad you rescued him." The man sits forward and leans to cough, his white hands are still shivering as they grip the arm rests of the leather chair. Mrs Turner passes Richie the mug. "Pour him another please," she asks. Richie goes to the farmhouse table and picks up the dusty bottle of old brandy. He pours a good measure into the mug and the golden liquid looks suddenly like poison as he passes it back to Mrs Turner. The old man grabs it from her and glugs it down. It doesn't take long. There's a change in him as the alcohol works into his system, the eyes begin to focus, he sits up straight and rubs his head. Richie sees clarity in this man where previous there was none. The Landlord behind the drink resurfaces, just for a few moments, before the brandy takes hold of him, and he is again stupid and drunk and angry.

"He was a bastard," says the Landlord. "I always said you shouldn't marry him. That's why we're in this mess now." Mrs Turner grits her teeth. This is how the day usually begins, with her father speaking as ill as he can of his son-in-law although it was he who introduced them all those years ago at the Driffield Show. "He was a greasy and evil robber and you were too in love to see it."

"That's not what you said at the time," says Mrs Turner. The Landlord looks at Richie because there is no one else to tell the story to. His daughter gets up to clear away some of the mucky plates from the kitchen table. The man's eyes have an edge of madness about them. "He's a pirate, I tell you. It wasn't a month since we moved in here, and Mr Bentley made me landlord that he robbed us – Christmas Eve it was last year. He took the candle sticks from the lounge and the silver from the kitchens, he robbed the money box and even the musket from above the bar – it was Dutch with a wheel lock action inlaid with mother of pearl. If I ever get my hands on that bastard, I will swing for him." Richie shoots a glance at Mrs Turner and she looks tired, as if she has heard this all before, and even more times than she can bear.

"Why's he called the Pirate?" asks Richie. He wishes he hadn't as soon as the words are out of his mouth.

"He's only got one eye," answers Mrs Turner from behind the kitchen table. Her voice is flat and cold. "The left one got knocked out when he fell from a horse, and he wore a patch so you couldn't see the hole."

"It didn't bloody stop him though," calls the Landlord. Mrs Turner walks over to her father and grabs the mug from his hand. Back at the table she pours in another good measure of brandy before returning it to him. It's a way to shut him up. The old man takes a sip and settles back into his chair.

"You were too good for him, Sarah," he says. Mrs Turner's eyes are cold and hard as she looks past Richie to the fireplace where the flames flicker.

"I don't want you to talk about him anymore," she whispers. "You just keep to your drink." Richie senses the tension on this thin and sincere woman.

"I'll help you clean up, Mrs Turner," he says.

CHAPTER THREE

It's nighttime and Christmas Eve proper. Richie has borrowed the big woollen cloak that hung on the back of the kitchen door, and he is outside at the log store behind the pub putting wood into two buckets. It's stopped snowing now, and the sky is clear with the frost twinkling across the fields and rolling hills. He thinks about his Nana back home in the little cottage opposite the Bay Horse pub in North Burton, far away over the cold forests and frozen streams. He's angry he's not there, she'll be angry with him too, because this is the night they spend together in front of the fire. She tells the same stories, of old fights she had with Walkington lads, tales of Christmas Carols up at the Pennyman House, and how Richie's eyes were big and round when he saw the bright lights of the starry sky as a baby; she tells of times that were good that are past and times that will be fine in the future to come. Richie sees the years ahead, for one day his Nana may not be there to tell those stories. He wipes his eyes with the back of his hand and picks up one of the buckets. It must be the measure of brandy he took ten minutes since that made him feel so. He won't have any more.

There's a figure standing in his way as he picks up one of the buckets full of logs. It's Mrs Turner. She is not dressed for the cold. Her face is stern. She must have followed him.

"What is it?" asks Richie.

"It's Mr Bentley in the lounge," she says. Her breath makes steam into the cold night air. She crosses her arms. "He's called us all to raise a toast around the fire at half past six. He mentioned you." Richie turns back to the firewood store and collects the other bucket of logs in his big hand. He sighs. Working in the kitchen here is one thing, but listening to that overbearing, privileged bore is quite another.

"Why me?" asks Richie. "I'm not a Skidby lad, I'd rather be at home with my family, Mrs Turner."

"I know, Richie, and I'm sorry. I'm sorry for all this, and that you've got mixed up in it. Mr Bentley is not well liked, I'll be honest. Neither is my father." Richie looks down into her thin face, her eyes are sharp and intelligent, she's too young to have to worry about all this. "I'm sorry you came by Skidby. Perhaps it would have been best of you didn't find my father at all."

"You don't mean that," says Richie. "Family's all you have in this world, Mrs Turner." This line comes from Philipson at the Bay Horse pub back in North Burton.

"Is it?" she asks. It's rhetorical. "I was married once, I still am, to that man my father calls a pirate because he has a patch over one eye. He wasn't a robber, Richie, and he was more a gentleman than my father and Mr Bentley, only he couldn't stand to live here in this place and have orders barked at him all day like he was a dog, so he ran." Richie feels guilty listening to Mrs Turner tell him her worries - as if he's some sort of inexperienced vicar. He swallows. He doesn't know what to say, so he asks a question, even though he's not sure the answer is any of his business.

"Will he ever come back?"

"I wouldn't have thought so, Richie, not with what my father has accused him of. Before we came here, he said we should go west to Leeds and find jobs in the town. I'm not a town lass, and I could never leave my father anyway." She looks out to the stars in the sky twinkling over the frozen landscape and then back to Richie above her. "I meant what I said before, Richie, when I said I needed a man about this place. You could do well here. You'd be paid and you'd have a future." There is the hint of something more, although Mrs Turner is not at all that sort of woman.

"I'm needed at home," says Richie.

"I know you are, your Nana is lucky to have you." Richie's Nana would never say this. If the old lass knew that he were here, outside and alone, talking to a married woman, she would give him a good telling off and a thick ear to boot.

From within the kitchen there's the sound of someone shouting, it's the booming of a man's voice. Mr Bentley calls out Mrs Turner's name like she's a sheepdog. Richie examines her thin face and the eyes staring back at him with a mixture of defiance and sorrow. She is trapped here, is this Mrs Turner, for Richie has seen this look on others before, it's the horror and the terror of being a slave.

In the front room of the Half Moon, it is half past six. The whole company that ate earlier is gathered. A big fire at the far end crackles in the fireplace with logs that Richie bought from outside, and the room is stuffy and warm with the smell of booze and overfed, perfumed toffs. There's the Allgood family from Northumberland and their three children with the serving girl that always accompanies them. Mr Bentley stands proud at one side of the great fireplace with his hand resting on the mantelpiece and his foot up on the hearth. Robert sits just behind him, and his mother is lost in the faces, as are his two younger sisters. The children of the group have been outside in the snow to collect what greenery they can. They have used twine to wrap leaves of holly around candle sticks and little branches cut from a fir tree stand upright in pots. One should decorate at Christmas, but not until Christmas Eve. Mr Bentley clears his throat and begins with the first line of Good King Wenceslas. He has a fine and strong tenor voice that holds the tune as he pounds out the first verse, others in the gathering join in.

Richie is here too. He stands at the back of the room near the bar with a tiny glass of sherry in his big hand. Because it's Christmas, Mr Bentley rewards the servants by letting them join in the singing and giving them a drink. It makes him feel better than it does them. The Landlord Richie rescued earlier has already got through most of the twenty-year-old brandy and sits on a bar stool with his face as angelic as a simpleton.

The carols continue with While Shepherds Watch, and Joy to the World. Richie knows some of the words but he can't hold a tune, so Nana says that in church he should just mouth the sounds and not make any noise at all - it's an insult to God when a lad can't sing.

After the carols, Mr Bentley stands in front of the great fire and tells the tale of the three wise men and Baby Jesus. Richie has heard this one before many times, and Mr Page, the rector over at North Burton, does a better job of it than the overconfident and arrogant Mr Bentley. He sets the scene badly, his voice does not have any other volume but to shout, and the characters in the story are wooden and hollow. Richie tries not to finish his sherry in case he gets given any more. His eyes stray to the other guests around the fire in the lounge of the Half Moon pub at Skidby at nearly seven o'clock on Christmas Eve, the year of our lord 1721. Mrs Turner sits on the arm of a chair next to an older woman with dull black hair. Auntie Bramble is in the corner with her eyes wide under the frilly skullcap and her hollow mouth open as she listens. Robert Bentley sits in an armchair with his face a little red from the drink and the heat, he is smiling at least - in a different life, Richie would be his friend.

After Mr Bentley has told the Christmas story and Jesus has been given all the gifts, he signals the end to proceedings by clapping his big hands together and saying thank you. It's a relief for Richie, he hasn't drunk all of his sherry and looks down into the little glass. It might be seen as rude if he doesn't finish it, so he drinks the lot in one go and the sweetness burns all down his throat. The ladies and children of the group stand and make their way into the side bar through a door, some of them drift upstairs and say goodnight. Richie peers through the square panes of glass in the bay window, and sees the snow coming down heavy outside again in the darkness. He would much rather be back in the cold cottage with his Nana, he feels a lump in his throat in worry when he thinks about her there all alone. At least the pub will be quiet in a few hours and he can get his head down and sleep in the kitchen, then, in the morning, to hell with the weather, he will walk back over the fields to North Burton on Christmas Day. Mrs Turner approaches him.

"I need you to give me a hand with one of the tables, Richie," she asks. He nods. "We'll drag the big round one through from the other room and set it by the fire."

"What's going on?"

"The gentlemen are going to play some cards." Richie's stomach drops.

This night is far from over.

When the cards and the drink come out, sense and intelligence quietly go on up to bed.

It takes ten minutes to set up the playing area. First, Richie brings in the round table and puts it in front of the fire with the help of Mrs Turner. She takes a fresh candle stick in a holder and puts it in the middle of the table. Next to the candle she places a big bottle of apple brandy and three glasses – the gentlemen take their seats. At one side sits Mr Bentley with his tomato red face and big stomach stretching the buttons on his waistcoat, beside him is young Robert with his half-grown moustache and ginger hair. Opposite them is Mr Isaac Allgood, the landowner from Northumberland way, and standing behind him is his daughter, Hannah. She looks to be in her early teens but acts older, she doesn't sit but stands at her father's back with her clever eyes darting around the room. The Landlord is not expected to play because he is already in the kitchen and falling over himself drunk. Mrs Turner has asked Richie to stand at the bar and serve the men while she tends to her father and puts him to bed. Richie wishes he had never seen the face of the old bloke peeping out from under the snow this morning. For doing the right thing he has been made to work the kitchen and cook for the guests, chop firewood, lose an arm-wrestling match, listen to carols and then the Christmas story delivered badly, and now, he must wait on these three men of money while they drink and gamble into the night. At first light, he will be out of the back door as fast as his legs will carry him.

"Barman," calls Mr Bentley. He shuffles a deck of cards in his fat sausage fingers as he looks across at Richie. "Bring some tankards of ale to go with this brandy." The tall lad goes back into the kitchen and there is Mrs Turner wrapping her drunk father up in a blanket in the armchair next to the fire. Richie was hoping to sleep there.

"They want ale," says Richie.

"There's a whole crateful of bottles under the bar there," she answers.

"Will they play cards long, Miss?" he asks. Richie's eyes are weary from everything he has done so far that day. Mrs Turner looks back at him with her own face full of fatigue.

"If you take the first shift, Richie, I'll do the whole night. Just give me half an hour and I'll take over. You've saved this day, Richie, and I'm asking you to help me a little more before this night is over. You deserve a crown for all you've done." She means this metaphorically. He won't get an actual crown. Richie nods. She is good with people, is Mrs Turner, she appeals to his better nature to get the most out of him.

Back in the lounge, Richie finds the crate with brown beer bottles inside. He fetches three out and carries them over to the gaming table where the men have not yet started their game of brag.

"I said we'll need tankards for that ale, lad," bellows Mr Bentley. Richie does not look at him but takes them back to the bar, opens them up and begins to fill metal tankards from the hooks with the rich beer. He hears Mr Bentley loudly talking a few yards away.

"Six foot four he says he is, bigger than my Robert, but it was my Robert who bested him at Indian wrestling, and it was no bother for him at all. Did you see, Mr Allgood?"

"I did," he answers, it's the first time Richie has heard the man with bushy grey white sideburns speak.

"Robert bested him easily." confirms Mr Bentley.

"If you say so," comes the dry reply. Mr Allgood takes a tankard from Richie and has a good long drink on it, the froth sticks to his long white moustache and he wipes it off with a napkin. "Now the women are gone, we can say what we like," he adds.

"Your daughter is standing behind you, Mr Allgood," says Bentley.

"Hannah is my bastard daughter, as I'm sure you've heard, she doesn't have the same temperament as the other lasses." He has a musical Geordie accent, but the words are stone cold. "She's here to watch and learn, no need to hold your tongue when Hannah is around." Hannah stands behind her father with her mouth pencil thin and her hair in a tight bun on top of her head. She looks at Richie and he can see white hot intelligence behind her eyes.

"You don't think my Robert beat him fair and square, is that what you're saying?" asks Bentley.

"I don't wish to offend, Sir, but asking a working lad to take part in such a game puts him in a difficult position. If he wins, he's in trouble, if he loses, he's a weak fool. This lad chose to lose to your Robert. You know that, and crueler still, your Robert knows it too." He's a wise man. Richie goes back to the bar and grins to himself so that the players can't see. He likes Mr Allgood – there's that Northumbrian straight talk to him with a good dollop of humour stirred through to make it sweeter and nastier as well.

"Would you champion this lanky six-foot working lad over my Robert, Mr Allgood?"

"Not at all. Your Robert comes from wealth and money, he has education, manners, and breeding. He's never had to work a day in his life, and just like your Robert can't lift a sack of coal, that tall working lad probably can't write his name. You wouldn't ask a fish to walk a mile and then laugh at it because it couldn't." Mr Allgood is correct. Richie cannot write. He can do his initials but that's about all. Nana says that reading and writing rob you of the bliss of ignorance. Mr Bentley is just self-aware enough to be insecure, and so he thinks Allgood is insulting him.

"Well, then," says Bentley, "let's get this lad to sit down here with us and play a few rounds of the brag, shall we? It's a fair game, you don't need too much skill or strength to play and I know working folk like to gamble as much as us of finer breeding." Mr Allgood takes a draft of his beer again and then sets it down with a thump.

"If you want to make the lad play for your amusement, that's fine, but it's Christmas, time for good will, not for petty games." Mr Bentley is all about petty games.

"It's settled then," says the fat man. He calls to Richie: "Bring up a chair, lanky barman, Mr Allgood will stand you a few pennies and you can play the brag with us. You can play brag, can't you, lad?" He returns from the bar:

"I know the brag, Sir," Richie answers. He does know the game of three card brag – he knows it better than most and plays in the Bay Horse when he gets the chance.

"Come along then, young Hannah there shall get our drinks and you'll play. What's your name, again?"

"Richie," he answers as he approaches.

"Right you are, Richie," says Mr Bentley.

There are men, and some women, for whom winning is the first goal. Perhaps it's not the winning they desire but the knowledge that they are better than others in some way. Such people miss the real sport that goes on around them, for competition is just part of the main game of life. You may win the race, but lose a friend or an ally; you may win an argument but lose the confidence of a lover, so when you play, you must weigh up if the winning or the losing will be of benefit to you.

Richie takes his place. In the years to come, he will play many card games on tables such as these, against men from all walks of life. Some he will play with a loaded pistol strapped to his chest, others with a full tankard of ale at his side. On this table, the new candle sends flickering light over the cards that Mr Bentley shuffles in his puffed-up hands. Richie sees that the other players have money next to their drinks. Robert has a slim tower of pennies, Mr Bentley a pile of mixed coins and Mr Isaac Allgood has a leather bag with a drawstring top. The older man opens the bag and takes out three pennies which he tosses to Richie.

"You can play till you lose them," he says. Richie looks down on the coins on the table in front of him. These pennies could pay for him and his Nana to eat for a week, and part of him wants to stuff them in his pocket and run, but he wouldn't get far in this snow. He nods in agreement as he gathers the money up in his hand.

Mr Bentley sets a penny in the middle of the table as the ante, and the others follow. He deals the rectangle cards with his swollen fingers – this is brag, a popular modern game that requires luck and a good degree of bluffing, hence the name. They play the first game and Mr Allgood calls to his daughter Hannah to fetch him more ale. Mr Bentley pours himself a large brandy but his son Robert shakes his head when his father offers him some. There are no drinks for Richie, but as luck would have it, he takes the first game, with a pair of threes – the best cards in brag. He rakes in the pennies and they begin again. Bear in mind that Richie does not want to win this game – the quicker he can lose the pennies given him by Isaac Allgood, the quicker he will be relieved by Mrs Turner and have a sleep in the kitchen ready to get back to North Burton at first light.

Richie has played with many decks of cards, and no two are quite the same. This deck is well made with stiff, new cards and gaudy pictures of the knave, the king, the queen has red lips and narrow eyes. Richie picks up an ace and sees that on the back of the card in the top right there is the tiny mark of a thumb nail line. This is card marking, and is common to those who play, you make a tiny indentation on the best cards so that you know what they will be without looking at the face – someone has marked this ace already. You can see what other players have and you can also play blind – but you won't really be blind because you'll know what you've got. The deck of cards over at the Bay Horse is so old and marked that you can't tell which is which anymore, but these cards are new enough for the marks to be of value. He loses the next two rounds and then a third before the next hand when he sees lined up before him, in the three cards he has not yet turned over, thumbnail nicks on each one. He looks at Mr Bentley and then Robert, then back down to his hand. Richie knows he has three aces. Mr Bentley must have marked these cards – this is his pub, or perhaps it was Robert, but he doesn't seem mean enough.

There's the game again. The decision whether to win or lose is Richie's. Now he knows the cards are marked he could play to win, and could, with time, win all the pennies from Isaac Allgood's leather bag – that's what Mr Bentley is going to do. Richie takes a deep breath and looks down at the cards on the table – his job here is to lose. He is a poor working lad with no money or education. He picks up the cards and sees the three aces blinking back at him. At the final round of betting, he throws the last of his pennies, and folds. Mr Bentley takes his cards but does not look at them as he places them back under the deck.

"You're all finished then, Richie," he says as if this was a foregone conclusion. "You've no more money left." Richie does not meet his eyes as he stands up from the table.

"Thank you for the game, gentlemen," he says.

"You know your place, lad, I'll give you that," says Mr Bentley. "You've lost to better men, and there's no shame in it. Now, back to the bar with you."

There really is no shame in losing to a man like Mr Bentley because it was never going to be any other way. Robert glances up at Richie in mild apology, he will be forced to sit there all night watching his bore of a father cheat Isaac Allgood out of however much money he's prepared to lose. This is the way the world works, there is God in his heaven, then Kings and Queens and men of wealth, they are followed by those who own land, shop keepers, pub landlords and even serving girls who live in posh houses; right at the bottom there are working lads like Richie Jackson, not worth even as much as a good hunting dog.

Behind the bar once more, Richie squats to the crate and fishes out another two bottles of ale and stands up. Hannah Allgood takes them from him and looks into his eyes.

"The cards are marked," whispers Richie.

"We know," she mutters back. "My father and I spotted them immediately." She does not at all seem worried by this information.

"I asked Mrs Turner about the dripping puddings at the meal earlier. We've never eaten them like that before. She says you made them – what are they called?"

"Yorkshire Puddings," he says. She nods.

"Mrs Turner told me the recipe. I wouldn't worry about the marked cards, my father is more of a gambler than Mr Bentley will ever be. I'll try those Yorkshire Puddings when I get back home, I'm sure they'll be popular." There is something about this Hannah that Richie can't put his finger on. At sixteen she will elope to Essex to become Hannah Glasse, and in thirty years or so, she will write one of the first popular books on home cuisine: *The Art of Cookery Made Plain And Easy*. Many of the recipes will be copied, but Richie's Yorkshire Puddings will be there along with instructions for curry, pilau rice and a cure for if you get bitten by a mad dog.

"Yorkshire Puddings fill folk up so you need less meat,"

says Richie. The girl nods again. Mrs Turner appears from the kitchen and comes over to the bar as Hannah Allgood takes the drinks back to the card players. She looks a little better than before.

"You can get your head down, Richie," she says. "There are blankets by the fire." He nods. It has been a very long day indeed.

It's late, well past five in the morning and the Christmas stars outside twinkle. The clouds have all blown away leaving a tapestry of jewels atop the frosty landscape. The sign above the door to the Half Moon creaks in the light breeze, and all is quiet on the little village street in the darkness and the cold. Footsteps creep silently around the corner to the backdoor, and a gloved hand checks the rapier at his belt under the heavy cloak. It's time.

Richie has been asleep on the floor in front of the fire. There's a draft, and the snoring of the old Landlord in the armchair, a mouse scurries under the table for crumbs and Richie dreams of Christmas feasts and his Nana wagging her finger at him in anger. He hears footsteps come into the kitchen and his eyes blink open. There's still some light from the embers in the fireplace and he senses danger somehow, so he pulls up the blanket and retreats to the dark corner with it covering him.

The figure of Mrs Turner dashes into the kitchen and there's the fat shape of Mr Bentley behind her carrying a lamp which he sets on the table. He hears her voice a loud whisper.

"You shall not do that to me, Mr Bentley."

"I shall do what I like," comes the reply. She is trying to get away from him, but Mr Bentley has caught hold of one of her arms and drags her towards him like she's a ragdoll. "Just a little kiss," he whispers, "at Christmas time - you know you want to." He pulls her close and Mrs Turner struggles at his strong grip. "You'll enjoy it," says the man, "best to just let it happen, lass. It'll be easier than if you fight."

Mr Bentley grabs hold of her round her middle as he tries to kiss her. She stretches her head back to keep her face away from him. This rich man is dangerous, and he is going to do something unnatural. Darkness clouds Richie as he watches from the corner. Mrs Turner whimpers as the man smothers her neck with his lips and tongue.

There are only so many times that Richie is prepared to let Bentley get the upper hand. It would be much easier for him to stay quiet and listen to poor Mrs Turner as she suffers, for Bentley is a man of wealth and power. It doesn't matter that Richie lives far away, he could have him charged with whatever he likes, and then Richie's Nana would be turned out into the cold without a home to live in. Despite this, Richie's big hand curls into a fist at his side as he moves out of the corner – if he plays this right, he can clobber Bentley on the back of his head and the fat bastard won't know who did it. Whatever the outcome, Richie will not let this happen.

Hang on.

The backdoor to the kitchen opens to the starlight outside and a figure steps through. He's tall with a long cloak and knee boots that click on the stone floor. The figure draws a rapier from his waist and the steel scrapes at the scabbard.

"Take your hands off her," he whispers to Bentley. His voice is iron.

"Who the bloody hell are you?" calls Mr Bentley. He does not release his grip on poor Mrs Turner. The man steps into the light and Richie can see his face. There's a short, cropped beard and black hair down to his neck; over the left eye is a patch. Mr Bentley frowns in disgust as he looks the man up and down.

"I'm your pirate, Bentley, come to take what is mine." Mrs Turner smiles wide when she recognizes the man.

"Thomas," she whispers.

"I'll have you for what you stole last time," snarls Mr Bentley as he pushes Mrs Turner away from him and steps towards this man who calls himself the Pirate.

"Caution, Sir - should you call for assistance, I'd be forced to run you through. Indeed, I think I would rather enjoy it." Richie steps back into the shadow of the corner once more. He'll let this one play out after all. Mr Bentley is now angry, he is a man who does not lose, and with the aid of brandy in his fat gut, he marches towards the imposing figure that holds a rapier deftly in black leather gloves.

"I'll tear your ruddy head off," he yells. The Pirate does not really want to run Mr Bentley through – it's not as easy as it looks, rapiers are good for cutting slices out of people, but in such a situation as he is in, he needs something more substantial to stop this bull cub who rushes at him. Bentley reaches out to grab the man, but the Pirate slides to the left and catches hold of the back of his collar. He drops the rapier and swings Mr Bentley like a pendulum in a half circle, releasing him so he goes spinning and then crashes backwards into one of the shelves. Jars fall on him from above and the Pirate moves in, brings his knee up into Mr Bentley's smalls and, as his body bends and roars out in pain, hits him a left hook in the temple that sends the fat man crashing into the stone floor of the kitchen. The Pirate looks down on the body, prone there on the uneven floor, he turns to his wife.

"I've come back for you, Sarah," he says.

"Where in God's name have you been, Thomas?" They embrace and the Pirate holds the back of her head in one of his gloves as she sobs.

"Your father paid me off, Sarah. Last Christmas, it was. He gave me ten guineas to go away forever and never come back. He said that I was poison for you and this pub, he said that he'd never seen you so unhappy, and so I took the money." Mrs Turner pulls back from him:

"Thomas, you're my husband."

"I took that money Sarah, and I took it to York and I sat down at the gambling table there in the King's Arms along the Ouse, and I played hard and I won. From those ten guineas I made fifty and I played bigger and harder than I ever had before, so that in six months I was a man with money and in another six, I had enough to buy a boat to carry trade up and down the river. I'm a man of something." Mrs Sarah Turner beams and her smile is bright and happy. "I have come back for you, if you'll have me." She throws her arms around him once more.

"I will," she says.

"We must ride. I would have come sooner but the weather kept me stuck at Market Weighton. My horse is outside." Mrs Turner looks around the kitchen in the lamp light, she frets when her eyes come to rest on her father, still asleep in his armchair.

"What of my father?" she asks, "What of Auntie Bramble? What about Mr Bentley here, knocked out on the floor?"

"You don't need to worry about them anymore, Sarah, they've never worried about you – if we ride now, we can be in York by tomorrow evening for the start of Christmas. Think of yourself for a change."

Richie steps out of the shadows and clears his throat.

"I'll tell them what happened," he says. They turn to him.

"Richie?" says Mrs Turner.

"I would have stopped Mr Bentley myself if your husband had not shown up." He means it too.

"What will you tell them, Sir?" asks the Pirate.

"The truth. That the Pirate returned, that he boxed Mr Bentley into next week, threatened me with his rapier, and then took Mrs Turner off with him on his horse." Mrs Turner beams again, and to see her face lit up is a joyful thing. Richie gives a wry grin. "The Pirate said he was heading south, to Lincoln," adds Richie. The man in the eyepatch winks his good eye at this tall and earnest lad.

"Who are you, son?" he asks.

"Richie Jackson of North Burton," answers Mrs Turner. "A good lad if ever there was one." The Pirate puts his hand in his jacket and pulls out a coin, a single bright crown. He flicks this across the room with his finger and thumb and Richie catches it in one hand. This is a lot of money.

"Merry Christmas," he says as he reaches down to pick up his rapier, the Pirate slides it down into the sheath at his hip then puts his arm around Mrs Turner. With a swoosh of his black cloak, they have moved out of the back door and into the very early morning. Richie goes to watch them leave and sees a white stallion waiting on the crisp snow outside. The Pirate mounts first and then pulls Mrs Turner up behind him, she puts her arms around his waist and her face is covered ear to ear with a wide and bright smile.

Richie stands and watches them ride off into the distance down the hill as the first rays of Christmas dawn shine on the Half Moon pub at Skidby.

He is a dead weight, but Richie manages to drag Mr Bentley through to the lounge and sets him in an armchair beside the fire. The man is mostly still drunk and the blow the Pirate gave him was not as savage as Richie thought. He builds up the fire and rubs his sleepy eyes while Bentley groans. Outside, the dawn of Christmas Day is starting and there's a blue sky beginning above the snow that fell yesterday. It's high time for Richie to leave, but he is not sure he can, not until the mess of what happened in the early morning has been cleared up and he has spoken to someone about it. There's a light cough behind him. Richie stands. It's young Robert Bentley with his floppy ginger hair and thin face.

"What's happened?" he asks.

"Your father's been hurt," says Richie.

"Did he take a fall again? Is he dead?"

"No, I think he'll live through this one." Robert gives a sigh of disappointment.

"He and Allgood played cards till the early morning. My father lost heavy to him. I left him drinking and went to bed. What did he do this time?" he asks. Richie is not going to lie, Robert seems like a reasonable and sensible lad.

"He went after Mrs Turner in the early hours, he chased her round the kitchen for kisses." Robert holds his hand to his forehead when he hears this.

"Did she hit him?"

"Yes," says Richie. Why mention the Pirate if he does not have to?

"Where is Mrs Turner now? Is she hurt?"

"She has gone, Sir," says Richie. She threw her thick shawl

around her shoulders in the early hours and left out the back door into the snow. I do not think she'll be back." Robert walks to the mantelpiece and looks down on his father asleep in the armchair with his beetroot face and huge fat gut under the belt of his pants.

"What am I to do with him, Richie?" he asks. This is a new experience. He has never been asked advice before.

"Stand up to him," he answers. "Nobody else would dare. You're bigger than he is, less drunk as well, and you could belt him on the nose if you had to." Robert breathes even and deep as he considers Richie's words.

"I will have to, the estate is falling to pieces with his drinking and bellowing, someone will have to take charge."

"It won't be easy."

"I know."

"Last night," adds Richie, "he was calling something about a Pirate before he fell into a shelf and Mrs Turner clobbered him with a rolling pin. Do you know what he would mean?"

"He will have been seeing things again," answers Robert. "Mrs Turner's husband, Thomas was known as the Pirate. My father says he robbed the place when he left, but I don't think that's true. It just broke Mrs Turner's heart. I do hope she is okay."

"She is a tough woman, Mr Bentley," says Richie. "Now, if you would excuse me, Sir, I must get myself back to my Nana at North Burton. She will be worried to sickness." Robert nods.

"Thank you for your help yesterday and last night, Richie Jackson. You are always welcome here in Skidby and in my house, whatever my father may say."

"Thank you, Sir."

"Just one thing before you go."

"Aye?"

"Did you let me win?"

"Win what?" asks Richie, although he knows the answer.

"When we arm wrestled, did you let me have the match?" Richie owes him the truth.

"Yes, I did. I am sorry." Robert nods in understanding. He

is not a fool like his father, there is even the look of a man who may be someone in the years to come.

"Merry Christmas to you, Richie."

"And to you, Sir."

In the kitchen Richie picks up the pack that he carried the day before from Kingston Upon Hull. It will take him a few hours to walk home in the snow and he should be back at least before twelve. The wrath of his Nana will be fierce, but at least, he has the crown that the Pirate gave him in the early hours of the morning. This will certainly sweeten the old lass.

He fits the pack over his shoulders and stands before the back door in the kitchen at the Half Moon. The fire is yet embers in the grate, the plates are dirty from the supper the evening before, and the Landlord sleeps with heavy still drunk sighs in the armchair covered in the blanket his daughter tucked him up in last night. Richie is glad he will not be here to see the chaos when they find out Mrs Turner has gone. He looks down and sees his battered boots and tatty pants, pulls the woolly hat from his pocket, and sets this on his head over his thick hair. With the crown he could buy a pair of stout boots and a new cloak, perhaps a pocket watch, and a bottle of apple brandy for Nana. It may turn out to be a fine Christmas after all.

As Richie goes forward to the door and puts his hand on the latch, he hears a light sniff from behind him somewhere in the kitchen. Meaner boys would make good their escape. Richie turns and hears the sniff again. He walks back into the kitchen and sees quickly that the noise is coming from the darkness of the corner. He walks towards it, and there, sat on a stool is the tiny body of Auntie Bramble. She's still wearing a frilly skullcap and her frail hands cover her face as she whimpers. Richie squats down in front of her so his head is level with hers.

"What is it, Auntie Bramble?" he asks. The old woman does not look at him, but wipes away silent tears from her wizened face.

"With Mrs Turner gone," she rasps, "I'll be put out into

the snow." She must have heard him speaking to young Robert Bentley. Richie swallows. This was a fact he had conveniently forgotten. Like the fate of the Landlord, Auntie Bramble's future is wrapped up with that of Mrs Turner. If she is not here, there will be nobody to help her. Richie is not worried about the drunk Landlord, he'll have to sort himself out, but this frail old lass is vulnerable. He feels his stomach drop as he reaches into the pocket of his pants for the crown there. There'll be no boots and no new cloak, no brandy for Nana and just the cold comfort of doing the right thing. The crown will not last Auntie Bramble forever, but it might get her passage out of Skidby to somewhere safer – it will be better than leaving her with nothing at all. He presents the crown to the old lass between his thumb and forefinger. Her big eyes look back at him in the darkness of the kitchen and she gives him a weak smile.

"I have a sister at Doncaster," she manages. "Will this be enough to get me there?"

"More than enough," whispers Richie. When she grins, he can see her gums.

Richie walks down through the village of Skidby on a bright but snow-covered Christmas morning. On either side of him, the thatched cottages wear a carpet of snow on their roofs. The going is medium to good as he strides down the main street with his breath making clouds in front of him. He'll cut across the fields to Risby and then Walkington and then North Burton. The air is sharp on his lungs and the heavy pack nips at his shoulders with the snow crunching under his feet. It's a fine and clear day. On the signpost that points to Risby, a red breasted robin comes in to land, Richie pulls at his woolly hat as if to tip it in greeting.

"Merry Christmas," he says.

#

You can find more tales set in the East Riding of Yorkshire here:

[The Great Frost: Three murders, a village lass, and a highwayman (North Burton Trilogy Book 1)](#)

The East Riding of Yorkshire 1709.
The tiny village of North Burton. It's March.
In years to come they will call it The Great Frost.
Meg and Nana know the cold will get worse – because everything always does. Meg's husband is away at war, the roof is about to fall in and Carrick, the big rector up at St Michael's, says the cold is a punishment for their sins.

When a wounded highwayman bangs on their door in the night, and they take him in, they don't realise just how much worse it will get.

[Richie Lad: A boy, his dog, and Dick Turpin begins (North Burton Trilogy Book 2)](#)

North Burton. The East Riding of Yorkshire.
Summer 1722.
When seventeen-year-old village lad, Richie Jackson, stops a midnight coach robbery, they make him constable of the peace.

He's not constable material.
An illegitimate son to that dead Turpin woman.
Six foot four with a big, daft hunting dog.
Nana says they only gave him a gun so he'll get shot.
After he saves the Pike lass, it looks like he might end up being a highwayman himself.
That highwayman.

[Nik the Swift: A kidnap, a highwayman, and vengeance (North Burton Trilogy Book 3)](#)

The East Riding of Yorkshire 1744.

Highwaymen still roam the coach roads. There's the smell of civil war brewing in the north.

Richie Turpin has one last errand to run before he goes to the gallows, again.

It's a Beverley lass called Nicola Sullivan, her father is a man of wealth and she's been kidnapped. Richie has promised to rescue her. That's not all. He knew Nicola's mother some twenty years ago in North Burton and there was something between them. Their business is not quite finished.

Nik will be a wallflower no more, for life on the road gives her freedom. If Richie can get her home to Beverley, she means to kill a man - her father.

Follow me for updates, snaps, and general chat!
https://www.chrisspeck.co.uk/
https://www.instagram.com/chris.speck.7528/

Printed in Dunstable, United Kingdom